The Ugly Duckling

To Alasdair

A PICTURE CORGI BOOK : 0 552 546135

First published in Great Britain by Doubleday, a division of Transworld Publishers

PRINTING HISTORY
Doubleday edition published 1999
Picture Corgi edition published 2000

3 5 7 9 10 8 6 4 2

Picture Corgi Books are published by Transworld Publishers,
61-63 Uxbridge Road, London W5 5SA,
a division of The Random House Group Ltd,
in Australia by Random House Australia (Pty) Ltd,
20 Alfred Street, Milsons Point, Sydney, NSW 2061,
in New Zealand by Random House New Zealand Ltd,
18 Poland Road, Glenfield, Auckland 10,
and in South Africa by Random House (Pty) Ltd,
Endulini, 5A Jubilee Road, Parktown 2193

Printed in Singapore

www.booksattransworld.co.uk/childrens

The Ugly Duckling
A Fiendishly Funny Flap Book

Jonathan Allen

Picture Corgi Books

Mr and Mrs Duck were proud of their five lovely eggs.
But they weren't so proud of egg number six.
It was splodgy and lumpy and very large.

By and by, the five lovely eggs hatched and five lovely, fluffy ducklings were waddling round their parents' feet.

Also waddling around their feet was something else.
It had hatched out of egg number six. But what was it?
It was far too large and lumpy to be a duckling.

The ugly duckling was sad.
He waddled on until he came to a mossy bank.
There was something just over the other side...
Was it his mummy?

Feeling very lonely, Ugly Duckling waddled away
until he came to a field of long grass.
There was something fluffy moving about in it...
Was it his mummy?

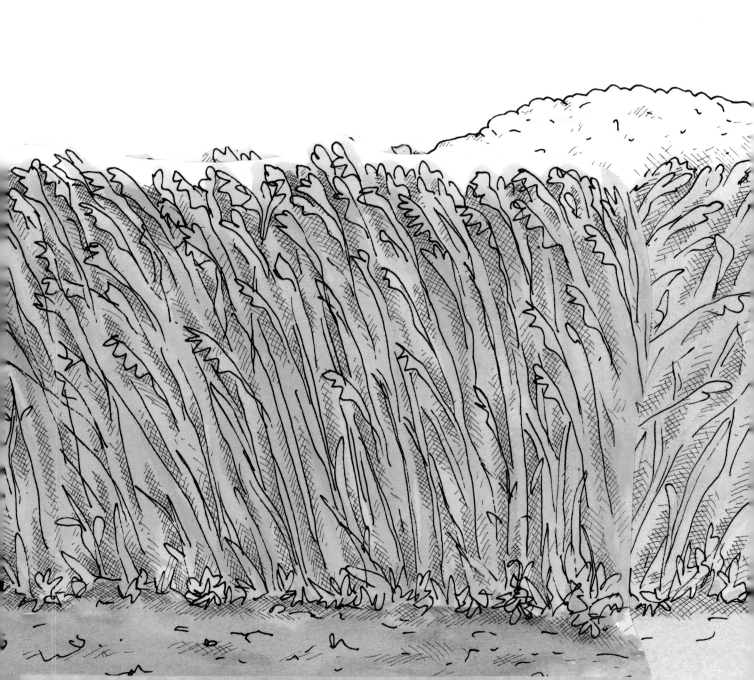

With a sigh, Ugly Duckling waddled off.
By and by, he came to a large hole in an earthy bank.
There was some kind of animal inside...
Was it his mummy?

Ugly Duckling wandered on feeling even more sad and lonely than before.
Just then, he noticed a handsome reddish animal in the cornfield.

This made Ugly Duckling feel much better.
He'd found his family at last...
Just then, he heard a loud rustling in the cornfield.
And it was getting closer!

The swan led the ugly duckling away through the cornfield to the edge of the lake.